CW00435607

(AN ADULT RETELLING OF THE LITTLE MERMAID)

'TIL DEATH DO US PART
(and adult retelling of The Little Mermaid)

'Til Death Do Us Part
(an adult retelling of The Little Mermaid)
copyright © 2011, Dianna Hardy

First published by Satin Smoke Press
via Lulu, December 2011
This version published by Satin Smoke Press
via Createspace, July, 2012
ISBN 978-1478270409

Satin Smoke Press
(an imprint of Bitten Fruit Books)
Surrey, UK

www.satinsmoke.com

For all of my soulmates,
wherever and whenever you are.

(AN ADULT RETELLING OF THE LITTLE MERMAID)

His eyes were the softest hazel. They always reminded me of sunshine and warm autumn days, when the leaves change from green to orange, then to brown. It was autumn when we got married. Autumn holds a kind of magic that humans take for granted … or maybe the magic was his. I guess if I had never known any better, I would not be missing him now, with an ache that kills me every day, over and over again…

The day you get married, is supposed to be the happiest day of your life. Dreams are made of such things. But I forgot. I could blame the witch if I wanted to – in fact I did, for quite a while after – but the fault can only lie with me. Being with him made me so happy – so very, very happy – that I chose to forget. I chose amnesia. If I had had any foresight into how my flippant choice would ruin him, I would have saved him the heartbreak. I would have forfeited my knowing him, my own selfishness, lived forever in the pain of unfulfillment, if it meant he could be spared....

'TIL DEATH DO US PART

"I do," I utter, trying hard to keep the tremble out of my voice, locking my eyes with his and using that earthly gaze as my lifeline. I swear, that sometimes, his eyes are solely responsible for keeping me upright, as if they save me again and again – what from, I couldn't tell you.

He slips the gold band onto my finger. The etching on the inside of the ring matches the one on his own and reads, *Simon and Aria.* It glides on as if it were made only for me. *Like Cinderella's slipper*, I muse to myself. I look at my prince.

"I now pronounce you, man and wife."

He beams at me. Those beautiful eyes that remind me of forests and woods, crinkle at the corners and he leans in without hesitation, his lips scooping mine up in a kiss that always seems like the first one.

How can I be this lucky?

I giggle erupts from my throat.

"Now the fun begins," he whispers in my ear.

My giggle grows louder and I feel like a school girl – what on earth am I doing getting married? I can barely take life seriously.

The congregation stand and applaud. The school girl within me blushes, and all at once turns into a queen.

It's perfect. The day is perfect, despite the thunderstorm battering against the old stained-glass windows. Storms unnerve me. I've always hated them. I used to have dreams – still do, in fact – of giant waves of some ferocious sea, tossing my broken body about as I try to escape, like a killer whale playing with a seal cub. I never do escape – until I wake up, that is – how does one escape from miles and miles of nothing but ocean?

He grasps my hand as we walk down the aisle, his warm palm, the only thing keeping me from legging it out of the church and running through the trees of the small wood that embraces the holy sanctuary. Even the thought of the storm wouldn't keep me from running today. I'm free. That's how I feel – utterly free.

He tugs at my hand as if he knows what I'm thinking. I suspect he does. He loves the wild child in me, he once told me. He loves the way I see the world through new eyes every day, the way I want to explore everything.

We walk out of the old doors and a bolt of lightning announces our departure from the church. It's so loud, I unwittingly look up and swear I see furious eyes in the sky, made blurry by the pelting rain. I shiver. I'm not superstitious, but I've always felt as if I am a part of nature, like a dryad or nymph, or some similar creature you're told about in fairy tales as a child. I have always thought that nature is something to be respected and nurtured, and I can't help feeling that some part of the planet is angry with me, although I can't hazard a guess at why that would be.

I grip his hand tighter, and he turns to smile at me, his face nothing but reassurance and love. The storm fades just a little.

He winks at me. "We'll be out of here soon, Aria. And don't worry about your dress – you look even more beautiful wet than you do with the sun in your hair."

His voice is low, his words loaded with hidden meaning, and I can't help the heat that creeps up my spine. The rain suddenly feels like a hot shower. Strange how the feel of rain on my skin should be so stimulating, when thunderstorms engender such a negative reaction from me.... Or maybe, I reason, it's the man holding my heart that causes the stimulation.

'Til death do us part...

The words wrap around my mind like soft, silk binds, and I cherish the imagery. Eternity can only be with this man – there will never be another who knows me so well.

"Simon..."

Reading my mind, he looks at his watch. "It's only just midday. No one's expecting to see us at the reception lunch for at least two hours." A wicked gleam flashes in his eyes in synchronicity with another flash from the sky. He brings his voice down a notch. "I want you so bad right now."

I gulp, suddenly aware of exactly how my body feels. Visions of us, writhing on the grass, in the rain, in our bridalwear, has me breaking out in a sweat underneath the white satin lining of my gown. Oh, god.

I want you too.

My eyes say what my tied up tongue cannot, and he sees it. He always sees me.

The photographer takes too long. Does he

have to be so picky about every little thing? At his instruction, our family and friends take it in turns to race the few yards to the gazebo where we stand. Everyone else waits patiently in the church's porch entrance, the small roof ledge doing little to shield them from the rain when the wind decides to blow in their direction.

After what seems an aeon, the photographs are finished and the guests leave, relief evident on their cold, smarting faces. I should be shivering, but I don't feel cold, only hot with a growing need I cannot pacify.

We wave our au revoirs. Then there is no one left standing behind the church but us.

One hand encircles my waist from behind and a soft, warm kiss trails the rain down my neck. Something between a sigh and a moan escapes me … *"I need you…"*

"Come on." Urgency colours my husband's voice. He leads me away from the church and we run towards the edge of the woods, the thin, autumn canopy offering a little cover from the rain, the rain itself, falling so hard it becomes our shelter from prying eyes.

I wonder if the happiness I feel is evident in my face. "We're both soaking wet – what are we going do?" I ask, my words light with laughter.

"Walk into the reception bare feet and wearing nature like a cloak," he grins. "It's our wedding day – we can do anything we damn well want."

Lips, hard, yet soft, meet mine; a hand fists my golden hair, still miraculously held up by spray and clips. No more. His pull at the already sodden strands sees to that, and I couldn't care less. "Strip me," I say, before I can even think it.

He stands back an inch, and looks at me in amusement. "How, exactly?"

I look down at the intricate buttons and loops on the bodice of my dress, then recall that there are even more ties that go around the back – I can't even remember how I got into the thing. "Oh," I say, not meaning to sound as disappointed as I feel.

He laughs out loud, no doubt at the expression on my face, then he's kissing my neck again, and hands are hauling up the hem of my dress. "The great thing about dresses," he mumbles against my skin, "is the easy access to the most important places."

His mouth finds my own, as his hand finds a very important place indeed. He rubs against me through my white tights, and I curse that I put them on.

A little sigh leave his lips. "You're so hot down here – are you wet for me, my little nymph?"

Hot? I'm burning ... I want him against me ... *now.*

"Off," I say, and I hope he understands the command because I am incapable of coherency.

He does. His hands race up in an attempt to find where the tights end, or start ... "How the fuck...?"

"Oh, shit," I moan. I remember that the corset of my bodice is low, and completely encasing the top of the tights which come up high at the waist. Frustration washes over me, and is audible in the next word I utter... *"Rip."*

Without hesitation, he digs his fingers into the sheer nylon and pulls, stretches ... and, god help me, my love for him swells. How lucky I am to have another who can give in to the moment without question.

Something rips, then rips some more; materials shift. Cool air caresses me between my legs, followed by fingers, long and sure. This time, my moan is one of bliss.

"Aria..." His voice carries a need he rarely lets anyone hear or see. He traces my slick folds, and I think I must be melting under his touch ... then he's pushing his way into me.

Yes! Fill me!

There are little flames lighting his eyes, matching the fire I feel within me as he strokes my insides, brushes my clit with the pad of a thumb, and it's pure ecstasy ... but, *damn it*, it's not enough!

"You..." I manage to stutter, between whimpers at the pleasure he knows how to build in me. "I need to feel *you...*"

"Then you shall have me," he whispers in my ear, with a guttural hoarseness that almost brings me to a climax right here and now.

With the arm he has circled around my waist, he tugs upwards. I take the hint and jump up, piggy-backing him from the front with my small form, my ankles locking together against his backside. His fingers push deeper into me at the sudden change of position, and the sound that leaves my throat is both loud and desperate.

Then we are falling – him onto his knees, me onto him. He leans backwards, and suddenly

I am straddling him and he sits on the wet grass. Inside me, he grazes against that sweetest of spots, and I cannot help but rock against him ... but I need more...

My fingers, surprisingly nimble in spite of the cold and the rain, undo his belt from its metal clasp. A button is popped, a zip is released.

My husband groans as I take him in my hand, all hard and scorching hot and wet at the tip. I lick my lips, feeling devious, despite my own body's yearning.

Oh, yes...

Shuffling down just enough, I take him in my mouth; heat and salt. The ocean roars in my ears and a memory ruffles against the edges of my mind, but I'm too far gone to probe further into it, and so is he, judging by the rumbling in his chest.

His hand is in my hair again, pulling me up. "Inside you, Aria ... now..."

I look at him as I move up along his body, both his hands now demanding I lay directly above him. He is beautiful. His full lips tainted rouge with my lipstick, his eyes, now a deep brown, glazed over with lust. I take a moment to bask in it, in our marriage, in our love. Some strange feeling fills my heart, and I feel overjoyed and anxious all at once.

"Aria, my love, are you all right?"

How can one man be so gentle? Why does gentleness feel so alien to me?

"I..." I cannot get the words out. My eyes well up.

Concern falls across his face.

"No," I say, placing a hand on his lips to hush him. "I'm fine, I just..."

I can't explain why this second is critical; why he must know beyond a shadow of doubt that I love him more than life itself. "I love you... No, I mean ... that's not enough ... it sounds so lame compared to what I'm actually trying to say. I—"

It is his turn to silence me, his thumb stroking my cheek. "Aria, I know. I love you too. In a way I never thought I could. In an icky way I used to laugh about with the lads—"

A guffaw leaves my lungs and I snort a bit through my nose, so unladylike, but it has him smiling at me in that way that is only for me.

The brown of his eyes darken once more. "Inside you, Aria ... please."

And I'm there, sliding down his hard shaft, sealing our marriage in the most intimate way. He groans at the sky and arches his back, mirroring my own reaction. We rock in unison and mini electric shocks of pleasure are racing up and down my body. Faster, faster...

"Aria, Aria, Aria..." he mutters over and over again, as if my name were his mantra of love.

It's a strange thing to hear your name repeated, quickly and to some kind of beat... Another memory tries to push its way into my mind, but an orgasmic wave is building within me and I become lost to nothing but sensation – the rain on my face, the swelling heat inside me, the man beneath my palms...

"I give you everything, Aria; I give you my heart ...'til death do us part."

The thunder roars.

My eyes fly open, and there is *his* face, angry and godly, behind the clouds. His eyes are the colour of the stormy sea and—

"Aria!" My husband's love fills me from below as *his* rage fills me from above. *It's him!*

Memories flood into me too late. I am torn in two, somewhere there is pain, but my body does not know it and catapults me into a climax I cannot stop. I am riding on pure love and ecstasy in front of *his* eyes.

Oh, god ... oh, no!

I smell my flesh burning before I feel the pain, and before I realise that a bolt of lightning has hit me in the chest, straight above my heart.

~*~

It's the same dream I always have. I am tossed and turned by angry tides, ten feet high. As always the dream begins to fade as I wake, but this time there is a difference: I ache. I feel as bruised and battered as my dream ocean would have me be. My chest feels so sore, I can barely breathe.

As consciousness rises, I realise I'm also cold ... and empty. So empty. There is a wetness on my cheeks – the rain ... no, wait ... the rain has stopped. I lick my lips and taste salt on them. Tears. I'm crying.

With effort, I peel open my eyelids which feel stuck together, and take in my surroundings. It's all hazy at first and I can't seem to see straight. It looks familiar. And then it hits me where I am: back at the beginning. I look down at my wedding dress, the sense of loss overwhelming beyond belief. The top of my dress is burnt, and an angry red scar lies across my left breast, over my heart.

More tears escape my stinging eyes. I remember everything, and I am lying among the very same rocks where I first saw him ten years ago – my prince; or at least, that was how I thought of him.

Still do, I tell myself, with a silent sob.

His T-shirt had been torn, his trousers twisted, his sand-coloured hair, matted to his face which sported cuts and grazes from the wreck. His yacht was in pieces. It had been the worst storm in over half a century around these parts. I had swum too far out, oblivious to anything but exploring new terrain. And then the storm had come in thick and fast, and I saw the yacht. *Prince* it had read upon its side. So naturally, not knowing the ways of humans too well, I assumed it to carry a prince.

With a groan, I rise onto my knees and find that I can't. My legs give way beneath me. Shocked, I look down. Yes, I still have my legs, although…

A fearful gasp leaves my lips. I shake my head. It is shiny – the skin on my legs – and on closer inspection, although I can barely make them out through my semi-torn tights, I can see tiny, translucent scales forming over my flesh.

No!

It can't be over, no!

"No!"

"What did you expect? That I would never find you?" The voice is close, his breath brushing hot against my ear. I turn, startled, and there he is, no longer intangible clouds, but corporeal mer-God. His hair cascades down over his shoulders, his jaw is strong and wide, his mouth set, his eyes as cold as the oceans he rules over; he is muscle-bound from his shoulders to the tip of his tail, and every bit as intimidating as any God could be.

Involuntarily, I shudder and wish I could hide it from his eyes.

He smirks – so cold, so very cold. "Did you not think I would turn every wave of every sea to find you, and then, when you were not there, did you not think I would climb the skies and scour the lands? Or did you *just not think?*"

I wince.

"Oh, Aria. For an entire decade, you hid well, you really did, but your little world fell apart when he gave you his heart. Wasn't that what that scum of a witch told you? That the minute he surrendered his heart to you, the spell would be broken?"

Fresh tears threaten to fall and I blink them back. He will not see me cry.

It is true. That is what the witch had said, but I had forgotten – another condition of the spell.

"I will give you legs," the witch had said. *"I will give you a human life, so you can be with your prince, but you must give me your memories in return."*

"My memories?"

"Yes. You must go into a new world, with a new mind."

"Well, I suppose—"

"There is one more thing…"

"Yes?"

"He must never give you his heart."

"But I love him!"

"And love him well you can, but he must never fall so in love with you, that he surrenders his heart. The minute he decides within himself

that he would give up his life for you, is the minute the spell is broken, and your humanity stripped from you."

"How will I know any of this? With no memory—"

"That is not my concern. You make a choice. You either be with your prince and forget about your own life, or you forget about ever being with him at all."

Never being with him at all – at the love-struck age of fifteen, as I was then – had seemed inconceivable. The thought of it had made me feel suffocated, and I had quickly decided that I did not need my memories – what memories were they anyway? Ones of floating around, trapped in a world I had never felt a part of. If I had known that he really would give me his heart, if I had had the maturity to see that I would be torn from him the second he did, and that he would suffer so for it, as he must be…

"You were stupid, Aria. Young and stupid. It was hardly a fair deal, was it? Witches are never fair, especially not sea-witches with their emotional dramatics – you should have known better than to bargain with one."

I may have been young and reckless, but

never for a minute did I ever doubt my feelings for him, and over those ten precious years spent with him in friendship, and later in love...

"I love him," I blurt out, and immediately wish I hadn't.

"You do *not*," he spits out, his eyes narrowing dangerously. "Childish games of 'let's pretend' do not a lover make."

"I do!" I am insistent and defiant, and I wonder where it's coming from – maybe I am stupid after all. One does not confront a God; certainly not when one is betrothed to him. "I had no memory of who I was, so you cannot blame a childish whim – I still loved him with no recollection of when and where I first saw him. And he loves me, for if he did not, the spell would not have been broken."

This is a fact he cannot argue with, and he is practically spitting fire now. I want to run, but my mutating legs won't move. I am disabled. Useless.

"It is not *you* he loves, but your human guise. Do you think if he saw you as you really are, with oil-sleeked hair, webbed skin of scales, gills for a neck, and your shimmering tail, that he would still *love* you?" The sky above him is growing dark and his eyes look like two whirl-pools.

I turn my gaze away.

"You are *mine*, Aria. You belong to me, and it is only to me that you will give your pleasure."

"You cannot force pleasure from someone," I throw back, angry with heartbreak, then real-ise my mistake. To a human that would sound like common sense; to a God, it sounds like a challenge.

Electricity crackles all over his form. I find myself shaking my head from side to side. Or maybe I'm shaking all over, from fear or rage I am not sure – maybe from both, because in truth, I *am* both.

He looms above me, blocking out whatever little light there is from the hidden sun, then falls forward. I stifle a scream as his hands fall either side of my head, quaking the rocks be-neath me.

"Aria, my *betrothed,*" his voice is deadly. "Say my name."

Petulant am I, for I have lost everything. I can feel the weight of the wedding band on my left ring finger, and it heightens my anger. I tighten my lips.

With a growl of anger, he lays one crackling hand under my breast and blissful heat shoots into me. I arch my back and scream in unwanted pleasure as an orgasm courses through my body.

"Say. My. Name."

I ache, but this time in a way this sadistic bastard should not be responsible for. The wedding band feels heavier now.

"Say. My. Name."

A sob escapes me, but I shake my head.

Another bolt of pleasure convulses through me, and I bite my tongue to keep from making any sound. I bite too hard; blood fills my mouth. Coming down from the climax, I realise I am gripping his wrists for purchase. A look of smug satisfaction falls on his face, and I am sobbing audibly now from exhaustion and shame.

"Don't you understand? You are of the sea, little one. I rule the seas. You are mine to do with as I please." He clenches my face painfully and forces me to meet his gaze. "Now, say my name."

I cannot lie – it's on my lips, but heaven help me, it is hazel eyes I see through my tear-filled sockets, not the unforgiving grey-green he would have me look upon. It is he who does not understand: a heart cannot be owned ... but when did a God ever understand that?

With a sinking feeling of despair, because I know that he will now break me, I shake my head against his hand.

A tempest of fury surrounds him and he rises, towering over me. He waves one of his hands in some sort of command, and a whirlwind manifests around him, growing thicker, blowing little chips of rock and stone into my body, some of them leaving nicks and cuts. His booming voice sounds out from somewhere in the swirl. "Perhaps this will be more pleasing to you, since you are so insistent on being human..."

The whirlwind fades and the despair grows within me. Legs have taken the place of his tail, and... I cannot look! I am trying in vain to scurry away, backwards, sideways, anywhere, as he lunges towards me.

"No!" I cry out, as hands take their hold of me. My hips are held down, the legs I had bargained my existence for, forced wide.

"Is this not what humans do?" he asks, with a sneer.

"NO! Please…" There is no humanity in this … and it is at this precise moment that I realise I have become human, maybe not in form, but truly I am one within. It is not unusual for godly beings to have their way with lesser ones – mythologies are littered with such stories. Many merfolk have stood aside and watched as their sons and daughters have been bound my duty to do things against their will, even encouraged. My own father nodded, mutely, many moons ago, when this deity, now bearing down on me, demanded his allegiance – he offered his daughter without a second thought.

Maybe I should be still; accept my fate. But I have tasted freedom, known love – I have had choice and learnt what it is to have a human heart, not just a compliant one. So I ball my hands up for all it's worth and hammer them into his chest as he forces his way into me. I cannot help my weak body, or the cries that leave me, or the orgasms he extorts from me as he tries to pound into my very soul … but I can help my heart, and he shall never have it, not even when I am nothing but consciousness floating on foam and waves, as is the fate of all merfolk – not even then shall he have it. My heart is the last human thing I own, and I vow that it will always remain so.

~*~

Ten years pass quickly when you are joyful, and excruciatingly slowly when you are mourning. Since I am in perennial mourning, I have come to accept, that time will forever be my enemy now. Simon is never out of my thoughts. I wonder if he is all right, if I hurt him beyond repair with what must have seemed my sudden disappearance. Does he think me dead? Did he go back to his life as a yachtsman? Did he race across the seas again? Did he find another to love? I cannot know. For a decade, I have been all but imprisoned since that tragic day that was our last. Knowing I would seek him out at the first opportunity, the sea-God, to whom I am now wedded, placed a permanent guard around me.

Mike Tysons of the mer-world, I think, wryly. Of course, no one down here knows who Mike Tyson is. But though I lost my human body, my human memories remain, etched deeply like an epitaph on a headstone.

Wherever and whenever I go, my two dutiful bodyguards follow. I have all but given up hope of escape. My only solace is that they do not much mind *where* I go, and that wretched God to whom I am bound has never forbade me any location ... because he knew. He knew I would never go back to those rocks. Once a place of innocent love and peaceful solitude, it is now always tainted with his violation of me.

So I don't know why, after all this time, today is different. But it is. Today I feel the anger I thought I had quenched – the rage that I thought I had successfully numbed. Maybe it's because the sea is turbulent with an impending storm – one that feels like it might be as big as the one twenty years ago that brought my prince to me, and changed my life.

I race through reeds and over corals, my guards in tow, a need I've not felt in a while, clenching my chest; I think it must be the need to be free – another fanciful whim I thought I had successfully muted. Today, I allow it to the surface, as I speed towards those rocks that both saved me and slew me. I can pretend, just for a second—

A movement catches my eye, below me to

the right.

What in the world...?

Another mermaid, trapped, caught in something, unable to move. I take it all in in a second – that and the shark approaching from her left. It is alone, and from the way it moves I can tell it is hunting. A mermaid would normally be too big a prey for a shark to bother with, unless it were starving, but a *trapped* mermaid...

I dive towards her, but am unexpectedly hauled back. Confused, I turn to face the guards.

Leave her, they communicate to me.

She's going to die! I try to get the urgency across, wishing I had speech and tone as my allies, but all I have are bodily movements and sound vibrations forming the foundation for telepathic exchange. Still, we understand enough.

Let nature take its course. It is not our concern.

Fury invades me. She's not a fish with a murky consciousness; she's a mermaid, a woman, with a *conscience* and individual thought. But even as I think it, I know they will not see it. Merfolk are cold creatures with a black and white understanding of complex things. And maybe the mermaid I ache to help also sees nothing beyond the darkness of the ocean depths. But I remember what colour is. A memory flashes in my mind, and I see a double rainbow over a traffic-jammed road, the tarmac slick with rain, an overturned car, Simon pulling over, me grabbing his arm... *"What are you doing?"*

"I need to see if I can help."

"How can you help?"

"How can I not?"

My human heart swells.

A mermaid's tail is her strongest asset, and without another thought I am somersaulting at high speed. I twist over at the last second, and ram my tail into the heads of both guards, then flee towards the trapped female. I know I don't have long – in front of me the shark is tearing through the water, behind me the guards will have already gathered themselves. I concentrate on the scene in front of me. If I could just see—

There!

A large rock lies on her spinal fin – it must have fallen from the side of the cave wall to her right. I'm not sure how I'm going to move it, but

33

the shark is there, and I don't have time to think about it. I charge forward at full speed and brace myself for the impact. For once, luck is on my side. The force of my sudden weight shifts it enough for the water to carry some of its mass, and with a little more pushing, the rock is falling away from her.

With two of us there and its potential snack showing able movement, the shark is now wary. I rise to my fullest and flick my tail at it in warning. It heeds it, and swims on.

For the first time in ten years, I feel like laughing. I feel light and buoyant, and the 'me' I used to be.

I turn to greet the woman.

A fist meets my stomach, knocking air and water out of me. *Damn it!* The guards.

I am grabbed and swung over a shoulder, no doubt to be taken back to *him* for punishment. I hope they leave the other mermaid alone – I can't see her from this angle…

Suddenly I am blinded.

What…?

It's as if someone is shining a torch in my eyes; everything is so bright and white, it hurts a little. The guard holding me drops me, and there is fretting around me, ripples of water telling me a story I cannot see.

The movements quieten, then cease, and the light becomes less bright, dimming to nothing, and...

Oh, dear god.

Everything has stopped. *Everything.* Except me ... and her.

The guards have been frozen in position, the water *is not moving* which was beyond weird, but even more eerie, is that I am able to move through the non-moving water, as if it is transparent and I am actually passing through it.

I look at the mermaid, and it is only now, looking at her properly, that I can see she is not a mermaid, but ... something different.

What are you?

She smiles, kindly, and I am taken aback. I have not seen a kind smile in too long.

I am old, is her reply. She reaches a hand out to me. *Come.*

Where are we going?

You decide.

Logic is telling me I shouldn't trust her; instinct has me wanting to fall into her arms; a decade of monotonous boredom has me yearning for anything different.

I put my hand in hers, expecting to take her with me as I swim, but instead, the world around us shimmers and disappears. It all happens so fast, I think I might be sick, but then it stops, or at least I think it has because it turns out my eyes are closed. I open them.

We are sitting on the rocks I love and hate, the cold wind greeting me.

Shit.

My eyes sting hot, but no humanness of my form remains, and I no longer have tear ducts with which to release my grief. Evolution did not make us to cry. Maybe I am the first mermaid ever to feel so much.

"You are sad?" asks my strange companion.

I nod, too afraid to speak, because I have not spoken in all this time.

"You saved my life. Thank you."

I nod once more, accepting her thanks, but I am breaking inside all over again. Why did I want to come here today? Why? I cannot do this. I glance to my left and the shredded yacht imprints in my mind. I little more to the right, and its beautiful owner lies unconscious, his head bleeding. I do not need to swivel around to see *him* pinning me down, his hands on my dress, ripping—

A sound like a sob escapes my lips – I need to cry, I need to cry, or I'll drown inside my own body.

"Sshhhh, little one, turn this way."

I do as she says. A warm palm is laid over my brow. Strange – all mer-creatures are cold.

An odd feeling passes over me, my eyes feel like they're being suctioned somehow – it's not entirely comfortable, and then the world explodes in an array of colours, so beautiful I gasp. I had forgotten just what human eyes were like. I look at her, astonished.

"Yes, I have given you human eyes – it's temporary I'm afraid."

I don't know what to say. I am overwhelmed.

"Are you a witch?" The sound of my voice is so foreign to my own ears.

"No. Although I do wield magic. I am an Elemental."

"An Elemental?" I am stunned. Elementals are things of stories and fables. "I thought you were a myth."

She smiles again. "And you are Aria, are you not?"

"You know my name?"

"Everyone knows your name, child. You are Aria, the brave. You are Aria, of the human heart. You know, the humans call a brave heart, a Lionheart."

Stupidly, I begin to giggle. It must be the shock. Or the grief. Or maybe I'm just going insane.

"I don't know what you've heard, but I am not brave. I am careless, selfish and stupid."

"How so?"

"Selfish because I wanted something I should never have had; careless because I never once thought of the consequences; stupid because I..." my voice breaks, "hurt someone I love very much."

"That someone ... would he be standing right there?"

Startled, I simultaneously turn and sink back into the water. He cannot see me like this. He *must not* see me like this.

And there he is, silhouetted against the setting sun, the wind of the oncoming storm, still far off, running its invisible tendrils through his hair. My breath is caught in my throat and I think I might choke on my lungs, because they are up in my throat too. Never in a million years did I think I would see him again.

He is only metres away, and I sink lower behind the rocks. He has not changed. How old must he be now? Thirty-eight?

His hair is golden under the sun. The last time I saw him, it was matted to his forehead with heavy rain as we made love in the woods by the church … *my husband*.

He seems like he is searching the waves for something … is he looking for me?

I clutch my chest, the lightning scar upon it all at once hurting. Above it lies my wedding band around a chain, no longer able to fit on my webbed fingers. *Simon and Aria.*

I want to call to him, shout out his name… Sod that – I want to take him in my arms and hold him forever. But I have gills for a throat, fins on my back and sides, my skin is scaly, slippery and cold. Doomed. He and I were forever doomed. What was I thinking? I have broken his heart as well as mine.

The day you get married, is supposed to be the happiest day of your life. Dreams are made of such things. But I forgot. I could blame the witch if I wanted to – in fact I did, for quite a while after – but the fault can only lie with me. Being with him made me so happy – so very, very happy – that I chose to forget. I chose amnesia. If I had had any foresight into how my flippant choice would ruin him, I would have saved him the heartbreak. I would have forfeited my knowing him, my own selfishness, lived forever in the pain of unfulfillment, if it meant he could be spared....

"Do you mean that?"

"What?"

"I know what you're thinking, little one. Would you really give up ever knowing him at all, if it meant he could be spared?"

"Yes," I say in a heartbeat, "I would."

"Then you *are* brave, Aria. It is unfortunate that time cannot be altered, despite what great scientists try to do. To turn back time, would be to turn back tides, to undo moons, to strip away oceans and the conscious thoughts of all that have them. If I could turn back time for you, Aria, I would … but I cannot.

"What time does do, however, and it does it best, is heal broken hearts."

I cannot think what she is saying is true. My heart has lain in tatters on the ocean floor ever since I was torn from the man now standing in front me. His name leaves my lips, and the tears from my temporary human eyes finally cascade down my face, for I have not uttered or heard the name in so long... *"Simon..."*

"Is it true, Aria, that you refuse to say his name?"

She is no longer talking about my love, and the fury I felt when I began my swim leaps up into my breast, as if battling with the pain of the scar that marks it. I turn defiantly to her. "I've never said his name and I never will. Not even on the day he wed me; not even on the day I die."

"The little mermaid who opposes the sea-God himself, no matter the hurt it brings her."

"There is no hurt anyone can bestow on me greater than what I have already felt."

"Simon!"

I was wrong.

With a sinking dread, I turn towards my husband and the voice that calls him, and watch as he takes a woman into his arms. Her hair is long and dark, she is tall, and I hate her – oh, how I do. She kisses his lips.

But he's mine!

He cannot love her – *he cannot.* I swear I see sadness in his eyes, despite his smile. Why is he sad if he loves her?

"Rain is coming," she says.

I look at the sky. It is unusual for a human to sense the storm so early on. What an odd thing to say. I turn my attention back to the woman who has stolen the only man I will ever love. Truly, I did not think the pieces of my still beating organ could be shredded even more, but there it is. Before, I was barely living; now, I must surely be dead.

"Aria..." the Elemental whispers in my ear. "I have something for you." She turns her hands upwards, and within each palm lies a pearl. One is golden, one is silver.

She raises the hand with the silver pearl. "Swallow this, and your prince shall be yours again. It will be done to him, just as it was done to you. He will have no memory of his previous life, but become a merman, and swim side by side with you, for as long as you both shall live."

She raises the hand with the golden pearl. "Swallow this, and you will die a true death. You will not be subject to the fate of the merfolk – you will not become one with the sea, but one with your own soul, as is the fate of humans. Swallow this pearl and you will have no choice but to let go of your prince, as well as everything you have known.

"Of course, you can choose to take neither, and continue on as you are. This is my gift to you for saving my life."

I'm trying to make sense of what she is telling me, trying to take it all in, but all I hear are the words, *side by side with you, for as long as you both shall live.* Hope flares in my tortured chest. This is what I want, what I have always wanted – him by my side. I reach for the silver pearl.

"Daddy!"

My hand freezes in mid-air. Did I hear that right? I turn once more and … I must be frozen through and through, for I can no longer move. And I cannot look away.

A girl of maybe five years old, with the same sand-coloured hair as her father's, comes bounding gingerly over the rocks, her arms outstretched. Her daddy – my husband – takes her in his arms. All trace of sadness is gone from his face. His smile is wide and true, and I've seen it before – during those moments we spent musing over the universe, or our future together. That smile is love and happiness and hope.

"Rain!" he calls out as he envelops her in a giant embrace. "Did you enjoy exploring?"

"I've got shells in my pockets; I even found a blue one."

Rain. He called her Rain. Clarity hits me as the vision of our wedding day fills my mind. The rain. Us in the rain. He called her Rain.

Oh, god.

I am smiling and crying, and crying and smiling. I am aching for him, sobbing for my loss, and overjoyed he has found happiness. Too much. I feel too much and I am done. Enough.

I glance again at the silver pearl. I conjure up the perfect image of us swimming side by side … and it is no longer there. Time has given him another life, another wife, a daughter he loves with all of his being. So instead I remember our wedding day, one last time. I wrap the image up with what is left of my heart, for I won't be needing it any more, and finally, I let it go.

I take the golden pill from the Elemental's

hand, place it between my lips, and swallow.

She is still smiling kindly, her face swimming in and out of focus in front of me. My body feels light. I look down at it and realise that I am turning into light.

"There is one more thing I can give you, Aria. You held your prince's name so sacredly, refusing any other – I can give you your own name in return. You shall remain Aria."

I have no idea what she means, and I have no idea why she is doing this – I've heard that Elementals are like the Fates of the ocean – it doesn't matter anyway. It's finished.

I take one last look at the man I love with the child in his arms, the light emanating from me, so bright I can barely see him at all.

"'Til death do us part..." I whisper.

And I am gone.

~*~

Twenty-two years later.

"Aria, are you done?"

"Nope," I mumble, concentrating on getting the final bits of dirt out of the lettering.

"I hope you're not becoming attached to that thing."

"Don't be an arse, I just want to get it clean."

"It's not every day you find a wedding ring with your own name on it."

I sigh. Mark can be a total dick sometimes. "It's just a ring, and I'm just doing my job. *You're* supposed to be helping me – I'm the junior, remember?"

He smirks. "Which is why you're doing the cleaning. One of the perks of archaeology."

I throw him a scowl. "Why are you not at the bottom of the ocean right now?"

He shrugs. "I'm waiting for Liam. If we find anything else, it'll be easier to collect it with both of us down there … and safer. I think there's a storm coming in. *You* should not have gone down on your own. I could get you fired for that."

"Give over – I wasn't even on duty. I was diving for relaxation."

"You hate the sea."

"I love the sea."

"No you don't. I don't even know why you wanted to study marine archaeology."

I remove the last piece of dirt from the ring,

and I feel ridiculously elated. Maybe I am becoming attached to the thing...

"I have a love-hate relationship with the sea. I can't explain it. That's just the way it is."

The door swings open and Liam walks in. Good. He's much nicer than Mark and we get on great, despite our botched attempt at a relationship last year. I smile at him and hold up the ring. "All done."

He returns the smile. "Great stuff. He's going to be here soon."

"I still can't believe you found the guy who owns it."

"Most of the time we don't. But every now and then, like in this case, there's a record of the find being a missing item."

And what a record it was. A police record to be exact, over thirty years old – an open and shut case. Wife goes missing on her wedding day after, apparently, getting hit by a bolt of lightning. There was speculation she was murdered by her husband, but no evidence of that could be found, not to mention, no body. The second scenario, assuming his story was true and she was hit by lightning, was that her body was catapulted some distance away and no one could subsequently find her, which is nonsensical and just doesn't happen. The final and most likely assumption was that she got cold feet and fled, and the broken-hearted groom simply couldn't admit it. Whatever happened the case was closed. And we would never even have heard of it were it not for the ring and the inscription in it, which exactly matched the inventory list for what she was wearing and carrying on her at the time.

"It's six o'clock already. Mark, we need to dive before it gets too dark. Aria, you sure you're all right to stay behind to meet him?"

"You will *give* him the ring, won't you?" threw in Mark.

I roll my eyes at him and turn back to Liam. "Of course," I shrug. "I am a friendless, twenty-one year old archaeology student with no plans tonight ... or any other night."

Liam leans in and plants a kiss on my head. "Only because you're devoted to the sea. Come out with me and Becky tomorrow. It's not just us, we're meeting a bunch of people down The Anchor."

I wrinkle my nose. "Can we meet at the The Woodman instead?"

Liam raises his eyebrows at me. "Is this because of that statue above the pub door?"

"I'm sorry. I know it's weird, but it totally creeps me out."

"Are you seriously telling me you won't set foot in that pub because of an effigy of Poseidon?"

I cross my arms. "You know I won't."

Mark's looking at me like I'm some weird new species of sea creature he's never seen before.

Liam just shrugs. "Whatever, babe. You're one of a kind." He grins. "Okay – meet us at The Woodman."

I throw him my best smile. "Thanks, I'll be there."

"Don't forget to lock up!" he calls out over his shoulder as they leave.

Like I would forget.

I turn my attention back to the ring. It's polished up nicely. I find myself smiling again, and then chide myself.

Silly girl. It's not your ring, no matter what name is etched into it … no matter how unusual your name is. That guy, Simon whoever, will be here for it any second and then it will be gone.

An odd sadness fills me and I push it aside. I rack my brains, trying to remember his surname. Tremaine, that's it. Simon Tremaine. I seem to remember reading something about him having been a yachtsman for Great Britain. For some insane reason I start to feel nervous. I must have had too much coffee today.

Standing up, I give myself a shake. Okay, time to tidy up for the night.

But my attention falls back to the ring. It even looks like it would fit me. And just like that, I suddenly can't never know whether it does or doesn't. It's stupid, and girly, and I just can't help myself. It's moments like this that has my mum tutting at me for my impulsive nature, which is exactly what she would be doing were she here.

Before sanity can find me, I reach over, pick it up, and slide it easily onto my left ring finger. Christ – it fits perfectly.

"Hello?" comes the voice, in time with a rapping at the open door.

Oh, fuck!

"Um..." I stumble as I turn, thrusting my hands behind my back. Grabbing at the ring, I pull at it. God damn it, it won't shift! This is *so* bad. "Hi," I say, and I'm momentarily stunned. For one fraction of a second, it's as if time stands still and I see myself running into this man's arms. Then the millisecond is over and I'm yanking at the ring again, trying to get it off. It went on easily enough, why the fuck won't it come off?

"I'm Simon Tremaine," he says, sounding a little flustered. Good, maybe he's as confused as me – that makes me feel better.

He holds out his right hand in introduction.

Right hand is good. Keeping my left behind my back, I take his hand and for some inane reason I catch my breath. Shit, I actually can't talk. And I can't let go of his hand.

He coughs. The spell is broken and I manage to flex my fingers enough for him to take his hand back.

Introduce yourself, Aria, tell him your name.

"Oh … I'm Aria Lawler."

He looks a little shocked, and then I realise why. My name is the same as the one on the ring – his first wife's name – and I'm wearing her ring and it won't come off. I'm officially a psycho.

So I do what I always shouldn't when I'm nervous: I laugh … *way to go, psycho* … then I babble. "I know, it's so weird isn't it. I'm the one that found it. I couldn't believe it when I read what it said. I've never met any other person with the same name as me, then I'm diving and I find this ring. It was my mum's choice – my name that is. She's Jewish, and in Hebrew, Aria means lion, but my father's Irish – I think she had to talk him 'round…" I'm not sure why I feel the need to justify my name to him, but I'm still trying to get the stubborn thing off my finger, and it's keeping him from asking where it is.

"So, where is the ring?"

Oh.

"Er…" In defeat, I realise that there's no good way to do this, so I look at him apologetic-ally, pray for forgiveness and bring my left hand out from behind my back. "I'm so sorry," I whis-per, embarrassment heating my cheeks. "I'm im-pulsive – it's a flaw."

He takes a step towards me and my dis-played hand. I sneak a look up, expecting to see horror or anger imprinted on his face, but to my surprise, his eyes are twinkling with amusement. And that's when I properly notice his eyes – the softest brown and so warm. Time does that funny thing again where it seems to stop, and a strange feeling floods through me.

Okay, I think to myself, *I recognise this – this is a crush, or lust, or something along those lines – which is really off, because this guy, as handsome as he is, must be around sixty…*

Not that younger women getting together with older men is unheard of…

"Impulsive?" he asks.

I nod. "It went on without any effort, but I can't get it off."

He clasps my left hand and touches the ring. My heart is beating in my ears.

"May I?"

I nod again.

He twists the ring, and gently pulls. Nothing. He twists it the other way and pulls again, a little harder. Still it doesn't come off. I want to die. I try to think of conversations that might make my stupidity easier to bear.

"So … your first wife's name was Aria…"

He looks up at me through long lashes and my stomach flip-flops. Oh, hell, I've got it bad for this guy – lust at first sight, or whatever – and I seriously need to get over it.

"What's your current wife's name?" Good question. A dose of reality.

"Her name was Linda. She died of cancer fifteen years ago now."

Reality sucks.

"I'm sorry."

He smiles. "Stop apologising."

Somewhere overhead, thunder rumbles. I tense up.

"You all right?"

"I don't like thunderstorms."

Something flashes in his eyes before I can really grasp it, then he's back to trying to get the ring off. I use this moment to study him in more detail. His hair is a sandy blond, with spatterings of grey throughout. His skin is tanned. I wonder if he still sails. Lines from his years in the outdoors map his face, but make him look as if he's lived life, rather than aged. I resist the urge to run a finger along them.

Another roll of thunder claps the sky, and this one makes me jump.

He catches me by the arms, and a gasp leaves my lips, which has nothing to do with the storm. For a moment we do nothing but stand there, staring at each other. If I just lean closer

—

Confusion flickers through his eyes, and he suddenly drops me. "I have a daughter about your age, maybe even a bit older..."

I wonder why he mentions it, then it hits me that whatever I am feeling, he is feeling too. It startles me how joyful I am at the thought.

But yeah, no kidding ... it *would* be weird to introduce a boyfriend older than my father to my own parents. They'd freak. And fuck it, I can't seem to care. I have my own flat. They wouldn't need to know for months and months.

I shake my head. I'm thinking like a crazy person.

When I glance back up at him, his brow is furrowed and he's staring at my chest. A blush creeps up my neck – why did I have to pick today to wear a low top?

Without moving his eyes, he steps in closer to me. I wonder if I should be mad at him for being so pervy...

"What's this?" he asks.

"What's what?" I reply, nervously ... he looks so intense.

"This." He reaches out a hand and it grazes the top of my left breast. Any minute now, I'm going to spontaneously combust. I look down, trying to hold it together.

"Oh, that's a birthmark ... ugly thing. It looks so angry. I usually cover it up." Why he's so intrigued with an ordinary birthmark is beyond me, but I can't say I mind his hand stroking my skin, so I say nothing. The same flash of something as before lights his eyes for the briefest of seconds.

Lightning hits the roof.

This time I scream, and I think he's yelling too. Something is falling – I can't figure out if it's the light fitting, or the whole damn beam it's connected to. I need to run, but my legs won't work, and a horrible feeling of déjà vu has me frozen to the spot, with it, the absolute certainty that I'm about to lose everything that I hold dear.

Arms encircle my waist, and I'm lifted off my feet and hurtling through the air. There's a crash behind me, and I land on something. I'm momentarily winded and can't quite get my bearings, until a groan sounds from beneath me. I realise what I landed on. *Simon.* "Simon!"

Is it possible for one word to change your entire life? I swear, the minute his name leaves my lips, something totally bizarre and inexplicable happens. It is as if I am suddenly standing in a vortex, or in the eye of the storm (although that particular analogy sends shivers down my spine). Everything around me becomes still and I am caught between two worlds which cannot exist without each other. I think it's a dream, or illusion; I think I might have hit my head, or maybe I'm dying, but he then raises his hand and strokes my cheek… *"Aria…"* he whispers.

At the sound of my name, those two worlds on either side of me collide, and my lips meet his. Time ceases to exist, and so, apparently does any logic that my mind is hanging on to. Logic would say that this is insane, every other fibre of my being says it's right.

His hand is in my hair, he is pressing me into him, his kisses as hungry as mine, and I am healing. I don't know what was broken, but without any shadow of doubt, I know that I'm healing. Slowly, I open my eyes, not wanting to break whatever magic has us captive.

"Oh, god!" I cry out in alarm, disentangling myself from him as red snares my vision. "You're bleeding…"

He pulls himself up to sitting. "I don't think

it's bad – I didn't pass out. I've hit my head worse before."

"We should have the hospital check it out." Reluctantly, I look behind me. A wooden beam and a smashed ceiling light lies on the floor, surrounded by more bits of wood. "I hope that's not a structural beam."

"It doesn't look like it, but we should get out of here."

I nod. "I'll leave a message on Liam's phone. I hope he had the sense to call off the dive."

"I think the storm's passed."

I look at him, surprised. "Already?" I glance out the window, and sure enough the rain has ceased. The sun, just setting, shines its rays far and wide, and every droplet of water upon land and tree sparkles gold. A double rainbow fills the sky to the right. I love double rainbows!

"Look!" I call out, excited. "It all looks so beautiful…"

The back of my neck prickles, and I turn around to find him standing up and staring at me. I'm amazed to see what looks like love in his eyes, but he quickly catches himself, and smiles. "So," he jokes, coming up next to me, "it seems that if I want to take my ring back, I have to take you too. I hope you like Chinese food."

"Chinese food?"

"It's all I have at home."

Home? I don't know what to say. Elation satiates me, and I don't care that it makes no sense. I think I love Simon Tremaine. To my embarrassment, my eyes fill up with tears.

And now he looks embarrassed. "That is … if you wanted to…"

Home.

I take his hand in mine. "I do."

(AN ADULT RETELLING OF THE LITTLE MERMAID)

About the author:

Dianna Hardy is a UK-based, multi-genre author of paranormal things, dark things, poetic things, sexy things, taboo things, and sometimes funny things. She mostly writes about witches, demons and angels.

Scorpio, hermit, loves nature, animals, walking barefoot, the woods after rain, and Summer days.

If you have to put her in the genre box, she writes about what you may consider to be "the paranormal", including paranormal romance, urban fantasy, gothic poetry and occult books.

Website: DiannaHardy.com
Email: dianna@diannahardy.com

Also by Dianna Hardy:

The Witching Pen
(Book One of The Witching Pen Novellas)

It's hard being the most powerful witch on the planet. It's even harder when you're a twenty-five year old virgin who'll lose all of that power the moment you sleep with someone ... that's why Elena's never slept with her best friend and flatmate, Karl, despite the true feelings they harbour for each other.

Elena's about to discover that there are even more difficult things in life to deal with. One of them comes in the form of a pen she discovers one day, a pen that allows anything she writes to come to pass...

Suddenly, it's not just her powers or her heart that's at stake, but her very soul, as a dream demon with a seductive pull uses the pen to try and turn her away from her reality, and from Karl.

But the pen is just the beginning. Everything Elena has believed in is a lie, and her world is about to fall apart...

Available now.

All details can be found at
www.thewitchingpen.co.uk

A Silver Kiss (Vampire Poetry)

A dark and daring addition to the literary world of vampirism, this is a collection of rhyming and freestyle poetry that explores the often taboo themes of power, possession and seduction.

Emotionally charging, each poem is written from a different perspective, be it the hunter or the hunted and inspires a deeper look into the psychology of the human mind and the darker aspects of human relationships and society.

Age range: suitable for older teenagers to adults.

Published by Bitten Fruit Books and available now.

All details can be found at
www.vampirepoetry.co.uk

'TIL DEATH DO US PART

(AN ADULT RETELLING OF THE LITTLE MERMAID)

Printed in Great Britain
by Amazon.co.uk, Ltd.,
Marston Gate.